Leo the Late Bloomer

BY ROBERT KRAUS · PICTURES BY JOSE ARUEGO

WINDMILL

PAPERBACKS

WINDMILL BOOKS and E. P. DUTTON

New York

For Ken Dewey

and

For Pamela, Bruce and Billy

**THE WINDMILL
PAPERBACK LIBRARY**

LUDWIG THE DOG WHO
SNORED SYMPHONIES

LEO
THE LATE BLOOMER

BUNYA THE WITCH

DADDY LONG EARS

THE KING WHO RAINED

THE TAIL
WHO WAGGED THE DOG

SHAGGY FUR FACE

HOW SPIDER
SAVED CHRISTMAS

SYLVESTER AND
THE MAGIC PEBBLE

CDB!

JUNIOR
THE SPOILED CAT

"COLLECT THEM ALL"

Text Copyright © 1971 by Robert Kraus.
Illustrations Copyright © 1971 by Jose Aruego.
This edition is published by Windmill Books and E. P. Dutton,
by arrangement with Windmill Books, Inc. Printed in the U.S.A.

SBN: 0-525-62312-4   LCC: 70-159154

Leo couldn't do anything right.

He couldn't read.

He couldn't write.

owl
Elephant
Snake
Plover
Crocodile

He couldn't draw.

He was a sloppy eater.

And, he never said a word.

"What's the matter with Leo?"
asked Leo's father.
"Nothing," said Leo's mother.
"Leo is just a late bloomer."
"Better late than never," thought Leo's father.

Every day Leo's father watched him
for signs of blooming.

And every night Leo's father watched him for signs of blooming.

"Are you sure Leo's a bloomer?"
asked Leo's father.
"Patience," said Leo's mother,
"A watched bloomer doesn't bloom."

So Leo's father watched television
instead of Leo.

The snows came.
Leo's father wasn't watching.
But Leo still wasn't blooming.

The trees budded.
Leo's father wasn't watching.
But Leo still wasn't blooming.

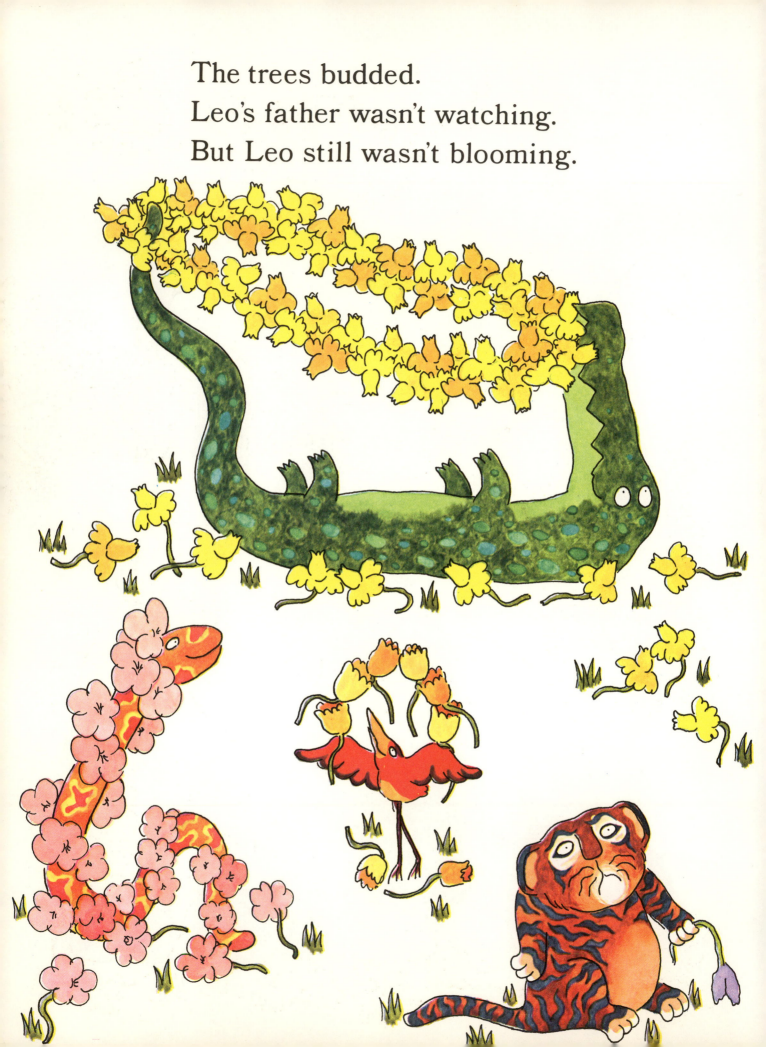

Then one day,
in his own good time,
Leo bloomed!

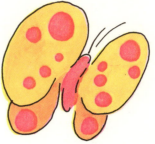

He could read!

He could write!

He could draw!

He ate neatly!

He also spoke.
And it wasn't just a word.
It was a whole sentence.
And that sentence was...

"I made it!"